June, 19

For Elliot, Shayna & Jonathan,

With love,

Tutu Arlene & Tutu kané Murray

Aloha!

Produced, published and distributed by
Island Heritage Publishing
First Edition, Tenth Printing - 1997
ISBN No. 0-89610-193-2

Address orders and editorial correspondence to:

ISLAND HERITAGE
A DIVISION OF THE MADDEN CORPORATION
99-880 IWAENA STREET
HONOLULU, HAWAII • 96701-3202
8 0 8 · 4 8 7 · 7 2 9 9

The typeface used in this book is Polynesian Laser™, licensed by Coconut Info®, and used by The Bishop Museum, the D.O.E., and Department of Hawaiian Studies.

Tales of

TUTU NENE

AND NELE

Written by Gale Bates
Illustrated by Carole Hinds McCarty

In Hawai'i, a Tūtū is a grandmother who is known for her stories and wise words. The Nēnē is Hawai'i's state bird and is believed to be the rarest goose in the world. Nele Nēnē loves to listen to her Tūtū's tales. When she finds a hole in the fence and escapes into the wild, her grandmother's words have a profound effect upon her survival.

The lives of endangered species always hang in delicate balance, and this tale will help young children appreciate their ongoing struggle to survive.

This book is dedicated to the men and women involved in the care and preservation of the Nēnē at the Hawai'i Volcanoes National Park.

As the sun set over the slopes of the great volcano, Mauna Loa, Tūtū Nēnē flew over the fence into the open pens in the Hawai'i Volcanoes National Park. The open pens provide a safe haven for young nēnē until they are old enough to survive on their own in the wild.

It was storytelling hour. All the young nēnē had been waiting anxiously for their grandmother, especially Nele, who was Tūtū's favorite grandchild.

"Tūtū, Tūtū, tell us a story," Nele cried eagerly.

“Gather ‘round, children.” Tūtū smiled and spread her large wings. “Long ago, many, many nēnē lived on our Hawaiʻian island. They were our ancestors,” Tūtū explained seriously. “They lived in kīpukas, which are the soft, grassy areas between the lava flow on the slopes of the volcano. In springtime, the nēnē tasted new plants and berries and spent their days roaming the island from the mountain to the ocean. It was a happy time. . . ” Tūtū sighed.

"Over the years, many of our ancestors were killed by hunters and wild cats. Then, one summer our ancestors were faced with a new danger: the fearsome mongoose! The mongoose arrived from a land far away, and he loved to eat nēnē eggs. But, most of all, he liked to attack young nēnē who could not fly. To protect the nēnē from the dangers of the island, the park rangers built the open pens for us." Tūtū paused and looked very carefully at all the young nēnē . "That is why you must stay here until your wings are fully grown!" she warned in a stern voice.

Standing up, Tūtū stretched her long neck. "Look children, here comes Ranger Kam with our dinner. Are you hungry?"

"Yes, yes," the young nēnē chanted as they followed Tūtū to the feeding dishes. Hungrily, they pecked at the delicious crumble. Nele ate 'til her tummy was full, then snuggling down, she dozed off dreaming of kīpukas, berries and beautiful new wings.

As the early morning mist rose above the trees, Nele was the first to wake. She walked along the boundary of the pen, eagerly pecking at the furry down on her small, undeveloped wing.

Spotting a piece of wire sticking out of the grass, she stopped to peck at it. To her surprise, the wire sprang up, leaving an opening under the fence.

"A hole!" Nele gasped.

She poked her head into the hole. “I think I can crawl under this fence,” she thought excitedly. Forgetting Tūtū’s warning and the story of her ancestors, Nele slithered her neck under the wire fence.

Wriggling and wriggling, she finally gave a big heave and scrambled through the hole. Nele scurried across the grass towards the trees.

Nele pecked into a plump, red berry. The tart, tangy flavor tasted delicious.
It reminded her of Tūtū's story about the juicy ʻōhelo berry.
Nele had always loved that name.

"Oh hello, berry!" she giggled, looking at the bush.

Listening to the soft chatter of birds overhead, Nele waded through a sea of ferns. She felt a gentle tickle on her underbelly and ran a little faster, laughing at the sensation. She skipped along, feeling very happy in her new world.

Suddenly, everything went black and Nele found herself falling through the air. "Help!" she honked loudly as she felt herself sliding.

Thud! She landed on a pile of wet moss. Slowly, she stood upright and shook her feathers.

"Well, I can still walk," she said, "but where am I?"

Cautiously, she groped her way in the darkness. "I hope there's a way out of here!" A teardrop slid down her cheek.

She bumped against something cold and screeched. "Oh, Tūtū," she cried. "Where am I?"

All she heard was the drip, drip of water on the wet moss. Slowly, she kept moving forward, her feet slipping here and there. It was hard to keep her balance in the dark and she felt quite dizzy.

Then she saw it — a tiny speck of light in the distance. Panting heavily, she ran towards the light. It grew brighter and brighter until suddenly, she burst out into the open sunshine.

"I made it!" she exclaimed. Nele looked back at the dark opening. She remembered the story Tūtū told about a tunnel made many years ago called a lava tube.

"Wow!" Nele exclaimed. "I was in a real lava tube."

The warm sunshine felt good on her back. Nele was glad to be out in the fresh air. She waddled along, hoping to find more delicious berries.
"Ugh, what a terrible smell," Nele gulped. "It smells like rotten eggs."
She sniffed the twirling mist rising out of cracks in the ground.

"Steam vents!" Nele exclaimed.
"The volcano is letting off steam! All of Tūtū's stories are coming true!"

She shrugged her feathers and hurried through the mist away from the stinky smell.

"Berries, berries! Where are those berries?"

Tchuk! Tchuk! Nele stopped. "What an odd sound," she thought. Maybe it's a bird, or a gecko, or even a mouse? It would be nice to meet a new friend. Using her beak, she pushed aside the green leaves of the shrub.

Nele froze and felt her feathers stand on end as she peered into the eyes of a fat, brown mongoose!

Tchuk! Tchuk! The mongoose twitched his nose. Nele tried to tear her frightened eyes away but the shimmering stare of the mongoose held her captive.

Tchuk! Tchuk! Slowly, she moved one leg backward. The mongoose stepped forward. Nele was terrified! She would have to do something! She couldn't fly! She would have to run!

And run she did! Over lava rocks, through the ferns and bushes she went, feeling the mongoose's hot breath on her tail.

Desperately, she tried to flap her small wings, but they just weren't ready to fly.

"I'll never make it," she sobbed.

Suddenly, out of nowhere came a loud honking sound. Nele looked up to see her Tūtū swoop down on the mongoose.

Tūtū spread her wings and stood erect, glaring at the mongoose. Nele shivered in the background. The mongoose stopped, his red, hot, beady eyes moving from side to side.

Tūtū fiercely flapped her large, powerful wings. Nele heard a long hiss. Slowly, the mongoose turned his furry, brown body and crept out of sight.

"Oh, Tūtū," Nele cried, rushing to her grandmother.

"Quick, Nele!" Tūtū warned. "Run home!" Still frightened, Nele followed her Tūtū to the open pens as fast as her little legs could run.

When Nele reached the pens, she was out of breath. Tūtū flew in over the fence. Nele ran up and down looking for the hole. Where was it?

All the young nēnē inside the pens were chattering and looking at Nele.

Then she heard it. . . Tchuk! Tchuk!

"Oh, no!" she cried, then sighed with relief as she realized it was only the sound of Ranger Kam opening the metal gate to the pens. Running towards him, she thrust herself through the gate.

Tūtū sat in her corner and Nele ran to her open wings. She was home at last. Safe!

Never again would she leave the open pens. . . well, at least not until she had her beautiful, strong wings and could fly.

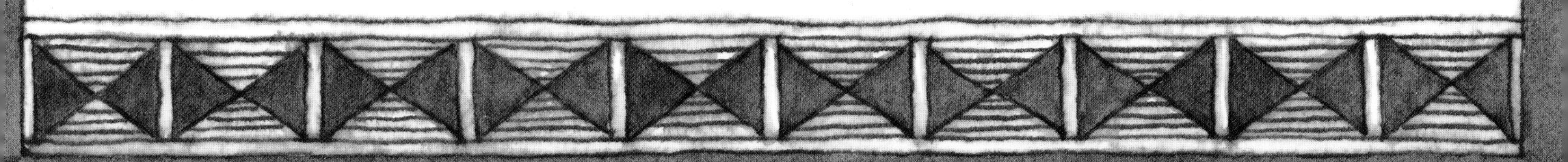

GLOSSARY

Gecko: A small, harmless lizard of the family geckonidae that is abundant throughout the warm areas of the world.

Kīpuka: A clear, grassy place or oasis within a lava bed.

Lava: The molten or fluid rock that issues from a volcano or volcano vent.

Lava Tube: A tunnel formed when the surface of a lava flow cools and hardens, covering the molten lava as it continues to move downhill. The lava in the tunnel eventually flows out the end, and leaves a space which is often big enough for people to walk through.

Mauna Loa: (Lit. long mountain). An active volcano on the island of Hawai'i. Elevation 13,680 feet.

Mongoose: A small, short-legged animal with pointed nose, small ears and long, furry tail. An active, bold predator who feeds on rodents, birds, eggs and sometimes fruit, the mongoose was introduced into Hawai'i from India to control rodents, the results of which have been disastrous for the nēnē . In India, the mongoose is noted for its ability to kill cobras and other venomous snakes.

Nele: Hawai'ian version of Christian name, Nellie.

Nēnē: Hawai'ian goose (*Branta sandvicensis*). Hawai'i's state bird is an endangered species found only on the islands of Hawai'i and Maui. A handsome bird with a dark head and striped neck, it is very approachable in the wild and utters a pleasing soft moan. By the time Captain James Cook arrived in 1778, about 25,000 nēnē were present, mostly at higher elevations. By 1950, fewer than 50 birds remained. This was the result of predators, grazing animals, hunting and other disturbances of the nēnē's habitat. Today, there are several hundred nēnē in the wild, mostly as a result of breeding the bird in captivity and releasing it. Man's help is vital if this endangered species is to be preserved for future generations.

'Ōhelo: A small native shrub in the blueberry family that has many branches and bears red or yellow berries which are edible raw or cooked.

Steam Vents: Openings in surface rocks through which steam from boiling ground water escapes into the air. Steam vents are common around volcanoes, and they often have a sulfuric smell.

Tūtū: Grandma, grandpa or any relative of the grandparent's generation. Commonly used in Hawai'i for a grandmother.